Dear Parent:

Congratulations! Your child is taking the first steps on an exciting journey. The destination? Independent reading!

STEP INTO READING® will help your child get there. The program offers five steps to reading success. Each step includes fun stories and colorful art. There are also Step into Reading Sticker Books, Step into Reading Math Readers, Step into Reading Phonics Readers, Step into Reading Write-In Readers, and Step into Reading Phonics Boxed Sets—a complete literacy program with something for every child.

Learning to Read, Step by Step!

Ready to Read   Preschool–Kindergarten
• big type and easy words • rhyme and rhythm • picture clues
For children who know the alphabet and are eager to begin reading.

Reading with Help   Preschool–Grade 1
• basic vocabulary • short sentences • simple stories
For children who recognize familiar words and sound out new words with help.

Reading on Your Own   Grades 1–3
• engaging characters • easy-to-follow plots • popular topics
For children who are ready to read on their own.

Reading Paragraphs   Grades 2–3
• challenging vocabulary • short paragraphs • exciting stories
For newly independent readers who read simple sentences with confidence.

Ready for Chapters   Grades 2–4
• chapters • longer paragraphs • full-color art
For children who want to take the plunge into chapter books but still like colorful pictures.

STEP INTO READING® is designed to give every child a successful reading experience. The grade levels are only guides. Children can progress through the steps at their own speed, developing confidence in their reading, no matter what their grade.

Remember, a lifetime love of reading starts with a single step!

For Dad, the best driving teacher
—K.L.D.

Visit us on the Web!
StepIntoReading.com
randomhouse.com/kids

Educators and librarians, for a variety of teaching tools, visit us at RHTeachersLibrarians.com

ISBN 978-0-7364-2982-5 (trade) — ISBN 978-0-7364-8127-4 (lib. bdg.)

Printed in the United States of America   10 9 8 7 6 5 4 3 2 1

DISNEY · PIXAR

Cars

DRIVING SCHOOL

By Kristen L. Depken

Illustrated by the Disney Storybook Artists

Random House 🏠 New York

One day,
Lightning McQueen
and Mater heard
a loud noise.
Hot rods were racing
into Radiator Springs!
Their motors roared!

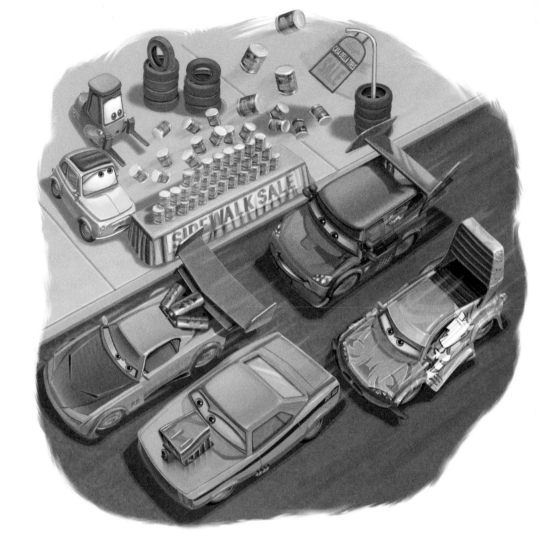

The hot rods zipped
past Luigi's shop.
His oil can tower
fell over!

They zoomed
past the Cozy Cone.
They splashed mud
all over the motel.

The hot rods
drove too fast.
It was not safe.

Sheriff stopped them.
He sent the hot rods
to driving school.

Lightning and Mater
were the teachers!

The first lesson
was about
traffic lights.
Red means stop.
Green means go.

Then Lightning told
the hot rods
not to drive too fast.

The hot rods
practiced driving
at the right speed.

Mater showed
the hot rods
how to pass other cars.
They took turns.
They used
their blinkers.

He even showed them
how to drive
backward!

On the last day
of driving school,
the hot rods
took a test.

They all got As!
They passed
driving school.
They could drive
in Radiator Springs
again.

The hot rods drove
down Main Street.
They stopped
at the red lights.

They drove slowly
and made new friends.
They had fun.

© Disney/Pixar

Lightning McQueen

But the hot rods
still wanted
to drive fast!

Lightning and Mater

had a surprise

for them—

the racetrack!

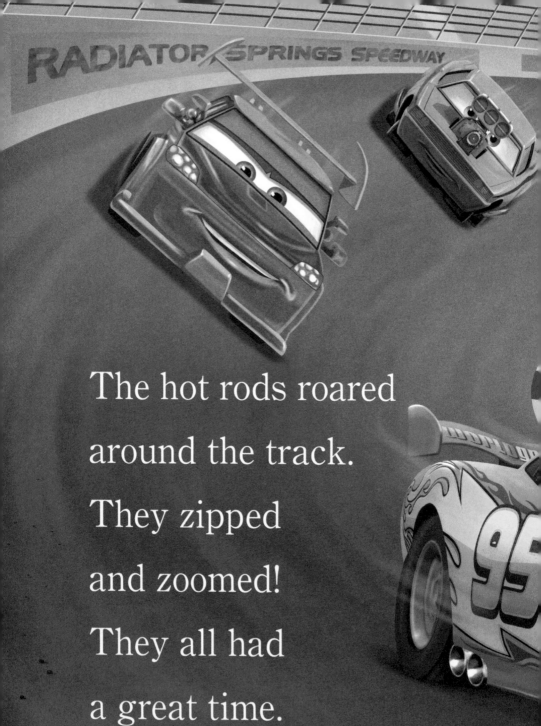

The hot rods roared
around the track.
They zipped
and zoomed!
They all had
a great time.
Everyone was safe.

The hot rods thanked
Lightning and Mater.
They were
the best teachers ever!

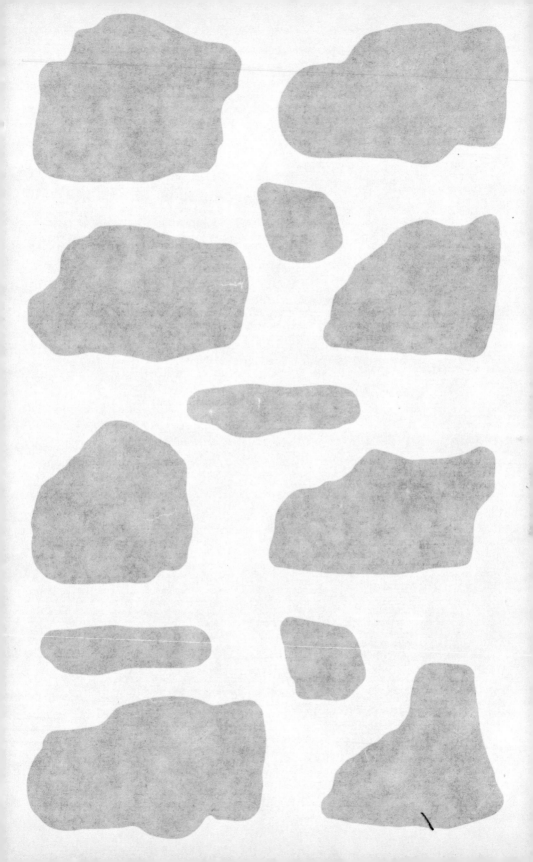

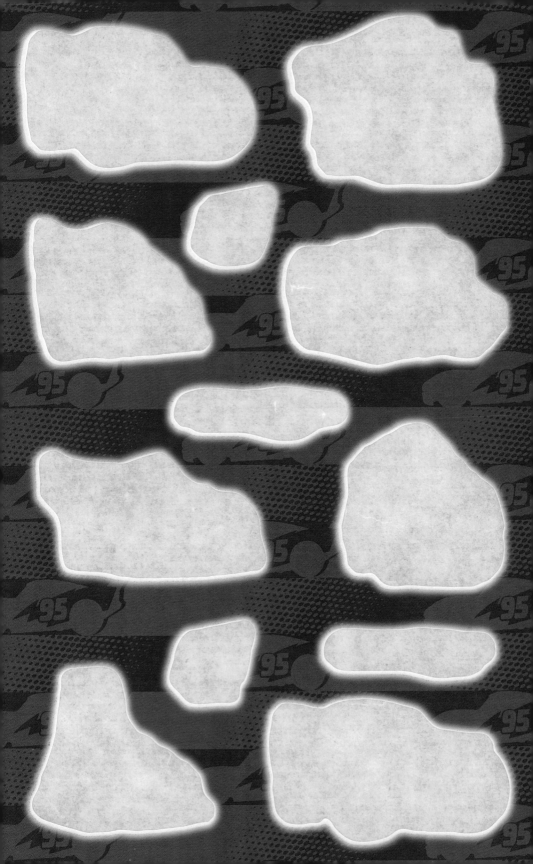

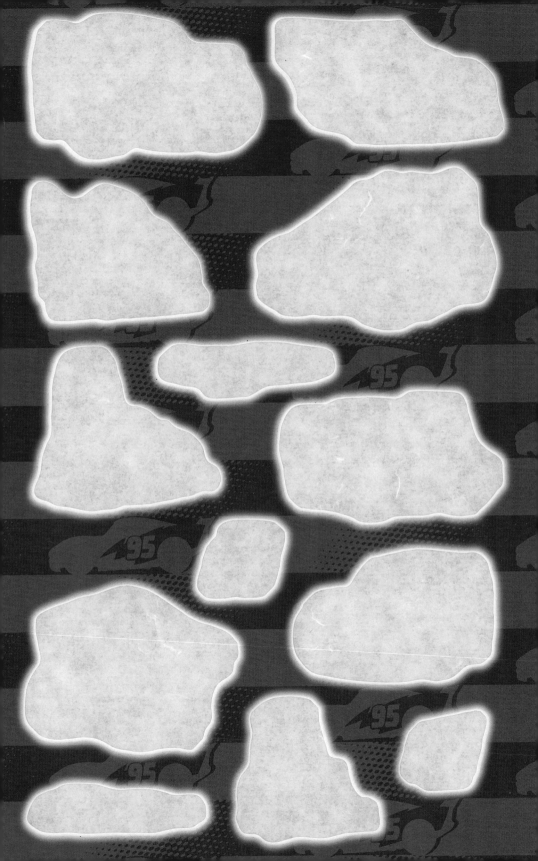